$15.95 B:T 9/00

W9-DAV-039

FARMER BROWN SHEARS HIS SHEEP
a Yarn About Wool

by TERI SLOAT   illustrated by NADINE BERNARD WESTCOTT

DK Ink

Dorling Kindersley Publishing, Inc.

For my husband, Bob,

who can spin a good yarn —T. S.

For Sarah —N. B.W.

A Melanie Kroupa Book

Dorling Kindersley Publishing, Inc.
95 Madison Avenue
New York, New York 10016

Visit us on the World Wide Web at http://www.dk.com

Dorling Kindersley books are available at special discounts
for bulk purchases for sales promotions or premiums. Special
editions, including personalized covers, excerpts of existing
guides, and corporate imprints can be created in large
quantities for specific needs. For more information, contact
Special Markets Dept., Dorling Kindersley Publishing, Inc.,
95 Madison Ave., New York, NY 10016; fax: (800) 600-9098.

Library of Congress Cataloging-in-Publication Data

Sloat, Teri.
Farmer Brown shears his sheep : a yarn about wool / by
Teri Sloat ; illustrated by Nadine Bernard Westcott.—1st ed.
p. cm.
"A DK Ink book."
Summary: Farmer Brown shears his sheep and has their wool
made into yarn, but after they beg to have it back he knits
the yarn into sweaters for them.
ISBN 0-7894-2637-4
[1. Sheep—Fiction. 2. Wool—Fiction. 3. Stories in rhyme.]
I. Westcott, Nadine Bernard, ill. II. Title.
PZ8.3.S63245 Ft 2000   [E]—dc21   00-021281

Book design by Sylvia Frezzolini Severance
The illustrations for this book were painted in watercolor.
The text of this book is set in 16 point Stempel Schneidler.
Printed and bound in the United States.

First Edition, 2000
10 9 8 7 6 5 4 3 2 1

Farmer Brown was shearing sheep,
Piling up a snowy heap
Of wool that filled his shed, knee-deep.

Clip-clip, buzz-buzz,
He took their wool and left them fuzz.

He filled his bags up, one by one,
With fleece, but when his work was done,
Clouds had covered up the sun.
The sheep saw all their wool in sacks—
"BAAA!" they cried. "We want it back!"

Soon the farmer's sheep were shivering.
They followed him—he was delivering
All their wool to Mr. Greene,

Who washed it out

And combed it clean.

Comb-pull, comb-pull,
He cleaned and carded all their wool.

Their fleece made such a fluffy stack!
"BAAA!" they cried. "We want it back!"

The sheep went running, cold and shaking,
Behind the farmer—he was taking
All their wool to Mr. Peale;

Who owned the finest spinning wheel.
Twist-hum, twist-hum,
What had their fluffy fleece become?

From fleece to yarn, it stretched and changed—
"BAAA!" they cried. "Our wool looks strange!"

Chilly sheep, with goose bumps, crying,
Rode right behind the farmer, flying
Down the road to Mrs. Muller,

Who changed the yarn from white to color!
Dip-dye, drip-dry,
The yarn grew bright before their eyes.

And while it dried upon the rack,
One sheep cried, "BAAA! Let's take it back!"

"What's this?" the farmer asked his sheep.
"You're tangled up from head to feet!
You're shivering cold and turning blue!"

So back to Farmer Brown's they flew.

He found his favorite place to sit.
Then Farmer Brown began to knit.

Knit-purl, knit-purl,
The farmer's fingers looped and twirled.

Crowded on the porch together,
Trembling in the nippy weather,
They watched him knit . . .
And when he quit,

He put a sweater on to fit
Each sheep, and then he buttoned it!

The sheep grew nice and warm again,
In brightly colored cardigans,
In patterns made of red and green
And all the colors in between.

Now each year, come shearing time,
The sheep wait eagerly in line
To feel the clip and hear the buzz,

And wear bright sweaters over fuzz.